Dinosaur Dreams

ALLAN AHLBERG · ANDRE AMSTUTZ

In a dark dark street
there is a tall tall house.
In the tall tall house
there is a deep deep cellar.
In the deep deep cellar
there is a cosy cosy bed.
And in the cosy cosy bed . . .

. . . three skeletons are dreaming.
The big skeleton is dreaming
about dinosaurs.
"I knew dinosaurs could run," he says
(in his dream).
"I never knew they had roller skates!"

Suddenly, the big skeleton is chased
by a very big dinosaur.
"You can't scare me," he says.
"You're just a dream."
"Grr!" growls the dinosaur.
"Help!" shouts the big skeleton.
And he runs away.

The little skeleton is dreaming
about dinosaurs, too.
"I knew dinosaurs could swim," he says.
"I never knew they had arm-bands!"

Suddenly, the little skeleton is chased
by a little dinosaur.
"You can't scare me," he says.
"You're just a fossil."
"Grr!" growls the dinosaur.
"Help!" shouts the little skeleton.
And <u>he</u> runs away.

The dog skeleton is also dreaming
about dinosaurs.
Suddenly, into his dream
comes the little skeleton
chased by a little dinosaur,
and the big skeleton
chased by a big dinosaur.

The dog skeleton
barks at the dinosaurs:
"Woof!"
And <u>he</u> chases <u>them</u>!
"Hooray!" says the big skeleton.
"Hooray!" says the little skeleton.
"Give that dog a bone!"

The dinosaurs run away.

The dinosaurs swim away.

The dinosaurs fly away.

But the dog skeleton finds them
and chases them again.
The dinosaurs don't look
where they are going.
Suddenly, there is a great big crash
and a very great big . . .

For some reason
(remember, this is a dream),

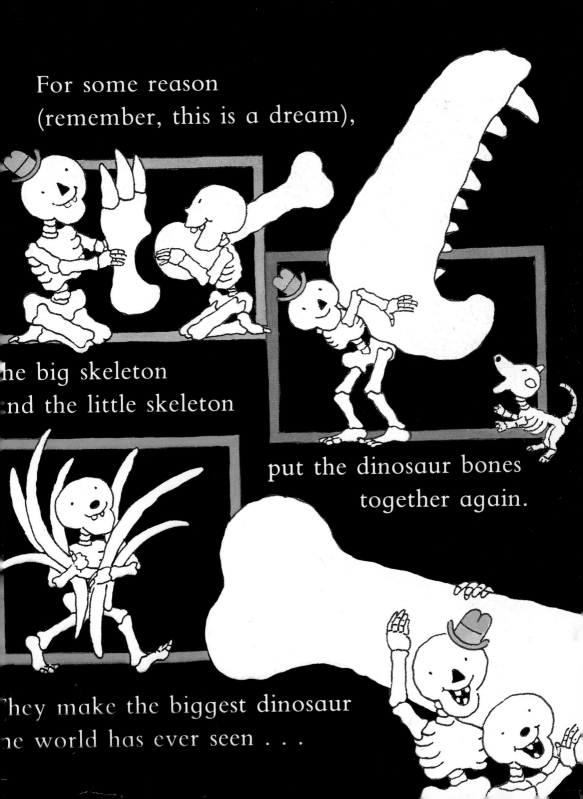

he big skeleton
nd the little skeleton

put the dinosaur bones
together again.

'hey make the biggest dinosaur
ie world has ever seen . . .

. . . and <u>it</u> chases them!

At last the big skeleton
and the little skeleton wake up.
They rub their eyes
and scratch their skulls.
They talk about their dreams.

"I had a dream about dinosaurs,"
says the big skeleton.
"You were in it."
"No, I wasn't," the little skeleton says.
"You were in mine!"

After that, the big skeleton says,
"What shall we do now?"
"Let's take the dog for a walk,"
says the little skeleton.
"Good idea!" the big skeleton says.

But the dog skeleton
isn't ready for a walk.
He is still sleeping.
He has a dream bone
in his dream mouth . . .

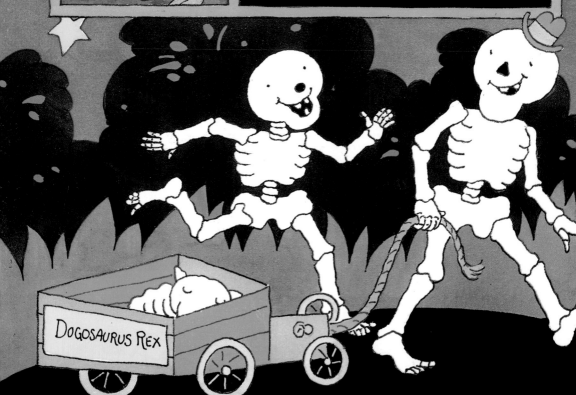

DOGOSAURUS REX

. . . and does not want to be disturbed.

The End

First published in Great Britain 1991
by William Heinemann Ltd
Published 1992 by Mammoth
an imprint of Reed Consumer Books Ltd
Michelin House, 81 Fulham Road, London SW3 6RB
and Auckland, Melbourne, Singapore and Toronto

Reprinted 1992 (three times), 1993 (three times), 1994, 1995, 1996 (three times). 1997 1998

Text copyright © Allan Ahlberg 1991
Illustrations copyright © André Amstutz 1991

The right of Allan Ahlberg and André Amstutz to be identified as
author and illustrator of this work has been asserted by them in
accordance with the Copyright, Designs and Patents Act 1988

ISBN 0 7497 0910 3

A CIP catalogue record for this title
is available from the British Library

Printed at Oriental Press, Dubai, U.A.E.